W9-CAW-922

Big Anthony and the Magic Ring

STORY AND PICTURES BY Tomie dePaola

VOYAGER BOOKS
HARCOURT BRACE & COMPANY
San Diego   New York   London

For
Paola Risposio
who introduced me
to Bambolona

Copyright © 1979 by Tomie dePaola
All rights reserved. No part of this publication may be reproduced or
transmitted in any form or by any means, electronic or mechanical,
including photocopy, recording, or any information storage and
retrieval system, without permission in writing from the publisher.

Requests for permission to make copies of any part of the work should
be mailed to: Permissions Department, Harcourt Brace & Company,
6277 Sea Harbor Drive, Orlando, Florida 32887-6777.

Voyager Books is a registered trademark of Harcourt Brace & Company.

Library of Congress Cataloging-in-Publication Data
dePaola, Thomas Anthony.
Big Anthony and the magic ring.
SUMMARY: When Big Anthony borrows Strega Nona's magic ring
to turn himself into a handsome man, he gets more trouble than fun.
[1. Magic—Fiction] I. Title.
PZ7.D439Bg   [E]   78-23631
ISBN 0-15-207124-5
ISBN 0-15-611907-2 (pbk.)

Printed and bound by South China Printing Co., Ltd., Hong Kong
H J L M K I

Printed in Hong Kong

intertime was very quiet in the little town in Calabria where Strega Nona (Grandma Witch) and her helper Big Anthony lived. People came to Strega Nona to help them solve their troubles. Big Anthony did his chores and tried to behave himself. And every morning Bambolona, the baker's daughter, came to deliver the bread.

One day the sun began to shine a little brighter, the birds began to sing a little sweeter, and the flowers began to bloom everywhere. Spring had come, and Big Anthony began to drag his feet.

"Anthony," said Strega Nona, "whatever is the matter? You're sleeping late. Your chores are half done, and every time I look at you, you're gazing into space and sighing."

"Oh, Strega Nona, I don't know what's wrong with me," said Big Anthony. "Everything in my head is fuzzy."

"I think you have spring fever," said Strega Nona. "What you need is a little Night Life. Why don't you go to the village dance tonight? It would perk you up."

Big Anthony sighed again. "The village seems so far away," he said. "And anyway, who would dance with *me?*"

"Bambolona, the baker's daughter, would," said Strega Nona. "Why don't you ask her when she brings the bread?"

"Who?" asked Big Anthony (for in truth he had never noticed her).

When supper was finished and Strega Nona was straightening up her cupboard, she suddenly stopped and said to herself, "Ummm. A little Night Life. That's not a bad idea. It's been quite a while since *I* went to the village and danced the tarantella."

Then she began to bang the little drawers open and shut, looking into each of them.

The noise startled Big Anthony, who was sitting just outside gazing at the moon.

"What is Strega Nona doing?" he asked himself, peeking through a crack in the door.

"Aha, here it is," said Strega Nona, holding up a tiny golden ring. "I haven't used this in years."
She slipped the ring on the first finger of her right hand and then began to sing:
"O little band, my golden ring,
  Listen to the song I sing.
  Make me look as I do not,
  And to the village dance I'll trot."

There was a puff of smoke, and instead of Strega Nona, there stood a beautiful lady, in elegant clothes!
Big Anthony could hardly believe his eyes.

Secretly, Big Anthony followed the beautiful
lady all the way to the village square . . .

and there he watched her dance the tarantella
all night long.

When the dance was over, Big Anthony
followed her back to Strega Nona's house.
There the lady sang:
  "O shiny band, my golden ring,
    Again the little song I sing.
    The dance is done, the moon does wane.
    Turn me back to me again."
Then she slipped the ring off her finger.

With a puff of smoke, there was Strega Nona!
"Oh," whispered Big Anthony, "if only I could
get that ring. I would be the handsomest man
in all of Calabria, and all the village ladies
would want to dance with me."

Big Anthony decided to wait for his chance—
which came the very next morning, after Bambolona brought the bread.

"Anthony, I must go and visit my godchildren,"
said Strega Nona, "now that it's Eastertide. Be
a good *ragazzo,* stay out of trouble, do your
chores, and don't drag your feet."

"*Sì,* yes, Strega Nona," said Big Anthony.

All day long Big Anthony waited. Finally, when the sun went down, he ran inside and rummaged through the drawers of Strega Nona's magic cupboard until he found the tiny golden ring.

He pushed it on the first finger of his right hand as far as it would go. Then he sang;
   "O little band, my golden ring,
    Listen to the song I sing.
    Make me look as I do not
    And to the village dance I'll trot."

There was a puff of smoke. Big Anthony rushed to the mirror and looked. The face looking back at him was certainly not his own. There stood a *Handsome* Big Anthony in elegant clothes.

"Aha," shouted Handsome Big Anthony, "and now for a little Night Life!"

When he strolled into the village, everyone
was dancing the tarantella in the middle of
the square.

In a second, Handsome Big Anthony was
surrounded by all the ladies there—young and
old, fat and thin, pretty and not so pretty. They
had never seen such a *handsome* man in all
their lives.
"Come dance with me," each of them cried,
pulling at his arms.

Round and round they went, dancing the tarantella.

So this is a little Night Life, thought Handsome Big Anthony happily.

After several hours Handsome Big Anthony
was beginning to get a little tired, but the
ladies wouldn't let him stop dancing.

"*Caro*," they cried, "dance with me! Me,
caro, next!" and they began to push and shove.

They pushed and shoved so much that at last
Handsome Big Anthony got scared.

"*Un momento*—just a minute! Let me catch
my breath," he cried.

But the pushing and shoving and grabbing and kissing only went on more. Handsome Big Anthony began to run.

The ladies began to run too. After him.

Handsome Big Anthony stopped and sang:
  "O shiny band, my golden ring,
    Again the little song I sing.
    The dance is done, the moon does wane.
    Turn me back to me again. *Please.*"
Then he tried to take off the ring, but it stuck
fast. *"Mamma mia,"* he cried. "What am I
going to do?"

Past the fountain, past the priest, past the sisters
of the convent on their way to prayers he
ran . . .

Out through the gate—past the goats—into
the countryside. "Me! Me! Dance with me!
Amore!" cried the ladies, close behind.

Handsome Big Anthony continued to run.
Again he sang the song, although he was out
of breath. Again he tugged at the ring. But
it wouldn't budge.
At last, he climbed a cypress tree. Up to the
very top.

Now he had nowhere to go.
"Help! Save me! Help!" he cried. And he
sang some more and tugged some more. But
it did no good.

The ladies reached the tree and shook it hard.
Shook and shook and shook it.
"Come down, you handsome devil, you! Dance
with us some more. With Maria! Concetta!
Clorinda! Rosanna! Theresa! Francesca!
Clotilda!" they cried.

Finally they shook the tree so hard that
Handsome Big Anthony lost his grip and flew
into the air.
"Oh no!" he cried. "Now they'll get me for
sure!"

He landed on his handsome big nose right in
front of a little house—Strega Nona's house.

And Strega Nona was home from her visit.
It didn't take her the time to blow three kisses
to see what had happened.

"Anthony," she said, "where did you get my magic ring?"

"Oh, Strega Nona, help me please. I only wanted a little fun. Just a little Night Life. I sang the song, but the ring is stuck. What am I to do? Here they come—they're after me! Please, make me *me* again."

Strega Nona opened a flagon of olive oil and rubbed some on his finger.

"Now," she said, "SING!"

Handsome Big Anthony loudly sang:
  "O shiny band, my golden ring,
    Again the little song I sing.
    The dance is done, the moon does wane.
    Turn me back to me again."
The ring slipped off his finger, and when the
puff of smoke had cleared, there sat—plain
Big Anthony.

"Where is he? Oh, where did he go? Where is that handsome devil?" cried the ladies from the village.

"There's no one here as you can see but me and Big Anthony," said Strega Nona.

Calling "Wait, wait, wait for us," the ladies rushed away. And soon they were out of sight.

"Oh, Anthony," said Strega Nona. "You will never learn!"

"Strega Nona, you saved my life. Never again I promise—never will I touch your magic," cried Big Anthony.

"Never mind, Big Anthony," said Strega Nona
with a smile. "There are other kinds of magic
in the spring."